Cyscoprime Publishers

An Imprint of Evincepub Publishing

Parijat Extension, Bilaspur, Chhattisgarh 495001

First Published by Cyscoprime Publishers 2020

Copyright © Aditi Agarwal 2020

All Rights Reserved.

ISBN: 978-93-90047-22-2

You Are Precious

Know Your Worth

By

Aditi Agarwal

Table of Contents

About The Book

The book is all about, knowing your self-worth it quides you to love yourself from every aspect, it is the combination of poems and articles, spreading love & kindness is the main objective of this book. along with self-love, it gives you the basic understanding of life & guides you to discuss and share your problems with your closed ones, also it lets you know the true meaning of friendship. It guides you the basic differences for example, between Ego and self-respect, it guides you to Be yourself but at the same time the book clears the difference between being yourself and being selfish. This book is a fusion of past & present, being nostalgic from past, and gives an overview to current situations & reflects present scenario.

About The Author

Aditi Agarwal is a student of commerce, currently persuing The Bachelor of commerce with honours (B.COM HONS.) She's passionate about writing, whenever she come across heart touching moments of life, she portrays all of them in the form of a unique edition of words in poetry. she strongly wants to bring about a change, and replace all the mindsets of cruelty with kindness, she just wants to spread love all around.

"we all are the writers of our stories, precised in words, that we deal with in our own little world."

_AditiAgarwal

Aditi Agarwal

Love Yourself

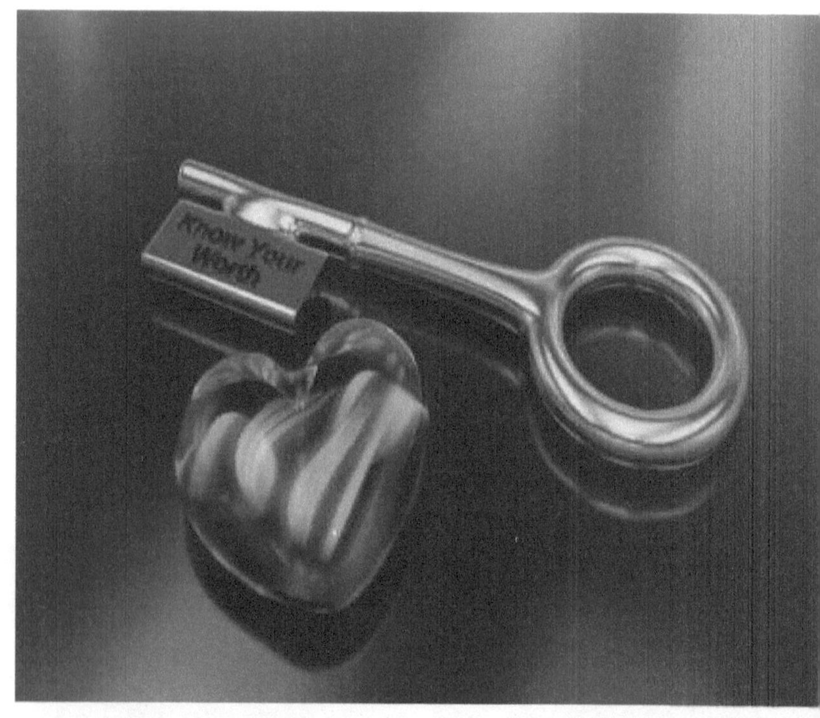
Know Your
Worth

1. *Make Yourself Yours Forever*

"NOBODY LOVES ME, I MAKE NO GOOD TO ANYONE IN ANYWAY, IT DOESN'T MATTER IF I WOULD NOT HAVE BEEN A PART OF THIS WORLD"

Ever felt that way? c'mon give me a high five & thank me later that i got to hear your inner voice. Chill Bud;

It's all about loving yourself, Find happiness within your ownself.

Find perfections even in your flaws. Make yourself feel special in every way you can; Never wait for someother person to make you feel that way. Never search for your happiness in others.

Tell yourself how important and worthy you are as an individual. SEARCH FOR THE REAL YOU, WITHIN YOURSELF.

Analyse, what all things you do for yourself. Understand, what all important roles that you play in your life for yourself; Then you will understand how valuable you are; that will make you understand your self worth.

Embrace your perfections & Do praise your imperfections too that will boost up the confidence and build a wall of positivity within yourself.

Tell yourself about the things that makes you different from others and gives you the impression of being UNIQUE.

You are blessed, if you realise what a wonderous heavenly creation god has made, in the form YOU.

"ACCEPTING YOURSELF IS THE FIRST STEP TO SELF-LOVE"

_AditiAgarwal

Aditi Agarwal

2. <u>Be Like A Queen</u>

Queens never chase;

let your beauty embrace.

 & by beauty I don't mean: fair skin tone, nice curves of body or an attractive face.

The perfect tinch of beauty requires: a pure heart, a peaceful soul & a strong sword of word.

which means; whatever you speak & promise make sure you actually mean it.

let others seek;

things from you.

& you need not peek;

into other's world.

Find perfections in your flaws,

& get ready to flaunt.

let others laugh like a clown,

you, take care of your crown. 👑

create your own thunder,

& let the world wonder.

make your personality glace,

let your enemies amaze. 😉

coz Queens never chase,

let your beauty embrace.

ALWAYS CHERISH THE BEAUTY THAT LIES WITHIN YOURSELF.

_AditiAgarwal

3. <u>The Flight Of Freedom</u>

Being a nineteen year old kid, by heart;
& a so called adult, by law.

standing on the threshold to depart;
& stepping away from the world of teenager.

wherein people expect us to be sensible & matured;
& living up to others expectations has to be ensured.
But the little heart screams to fly high
& enjoy being yourself.
Little did the heart know, challenges were more to face and yet to come further.
The challenge of differentiation & comparison between you & your friends or siblings.
coz for them being of same age-group may be means: same interest, same qualities, same work, same mindset or maybe same profession.

Fighting between the war of being yourself and being what exactly others want you to be.

Learn to FIGHT FOR THE FLIGHT OF FREEDOM.

otherwise, either you will loose your inner kid within yourself forever or you will become the best obedient & disciplined, so called "child", by agreeing to everything people want you to be like.

Being in that case always, try to listen the inner voice within yourself, because at last it's we who enables to understand our self first, instead of explaining things to others & expecting them to understand us.

In fulfillment of obligations that are imposed by others on us, Never loose yourself; try to find the real You within yourself.

coz you need not change a thing about yourself, Be the way you are.

GET READY TO FLY HIGH; IN THE SKY.

_AditiAgarwal

Aditi Agarwal

4. *Dear Girls*

You don't have to look beautiful for a day;
Coz every girl is beautiful in her own way.

Shoot on to all those teasy comments
through a trigger;
& just don't care even if you don't have
a nice figure.

You don't have to bother to bother to what people say!
Coz every girl is beautiful in her own way.

Go to a nearby park;
Sing there like a lark,
& just don't care even
if your complexion is
a bit dark.

Just put on a nice hat
& do not bother even if you are a bit fat.

Fax all those uneasy comments into the dustbin;
Without paying tax,

& just don't care even if you wear specs.

Because girls don't have to look beautiful for a day;
As every girl is beautiful in her own way!

13

_AditiAgarwal

5. <u>Stop Quitting Life</u>

Now a days it has become a trend; that if you can't handle your life, so just give upon it and quit! It is so easy to give up on life but facing hurdles and going through the main roots of the problens is quite difficult.Life is as easy as riding a bicycle until and unless you do not know how to handle it and make a perfect balance even when going through the hurdles.Life is lived once; and the one's who love their life, they crave for some more moments to live, to which you yourself wish to give upon.Sometimes; it really gets difficult for you to express yourself that you burst out crying, but the other person still does not understands anything or does not even listen to you but quiting on your life is not the only solution to get rid of your problems, you will have to face it until you break it into pieces; "break" not your heart but the reason or the root cause of your problem.You don't have to be sad for any reason; the one that made you sad would not even know that upto what an extent he/she has hurt you that made you go through such a depression that you felt like giving up on your life.So the best way is to forget and forgive; because today or the other day karma will in itself come through their way, you don't have to do anything, just sit back and smile.Take the advantage of your life to the fullest; each and every moment of your life is very precious and most importantly the smile to your face, is as precious as the drop of water onto a barren land.

_AditiAgarwal

6. _Girl As A Pearl_

She took birth,
not knowing her worth.
The first day, when she cried,
many were beside.
"But today when she cries,
those "many" are only there to
misguide.
she tears up in disguise,
hearing advices which her heart
denies".

"Now, she knew her worth,
knowing the significance of her birth".
She then made a promise to herself,
to never doubt her abilities;
because she knew, what she deserves,
it is reserved for her own self.

she again and again cried,
but these tears always dried;
& finally, one fine day,
she achieved the sunrise 🌞 of
prosperity,
in her life.

"All what you need to have is confidence,

that will give you the courage, i.e immense.

Never let yourself down in anyway,

practice loving yourself, every day."

_AditiAgarwal

Aditi Agarwal

7. <u>Self Importance</u>

with the word itself it's very clear that self importance is for your ownself.

The significance that you carry within yourself for your ownself is self importance.

That determines you should feel free to execute things the way you want to; feel free to make things and situations favour you.

Each time you try doing something new, you will come across many challanges in different ways, there will always be people discouraging you, a group of people who would act good at your face but at your back, will not leave any chance of making fun amongst others; Don't let this disgust discourage you , instead take this as a blessing in disguise, coz if it's your happiness that makes them feel sad; better you know that you are at higher place; & you have got your standards raised.

_AditiAgarwal

Aditi Agarwal

8. <u>Believe In Yourself</u>

Believe in yourself for a cause,

not for applause.

Believe in yourself to express,

not to impress.

Believe in yourself to achieve an eve,

to relieve yourself.

Believe in yourself & perceive gratitude,

to defeat the negative attitude.

Believe in yourself and have capacity,

to hold the dignity.

Believe in yourself to discard negativity,

and gain prosperity.

_AditiAgarwal

Aditi Agarwal

Discuss Problems With Others

9. *Developing Friendly Relationship With Parents*

From hearing taunts;

till dusk and dawn,

To sharing thoughts & forgone,

while sitting in the lawn along with your mom.

crossing teenage while fighting between emotional traumas and agression,

To defeating & overcoming all such depressions.

From being quiet & having fight,

To developing friendly relations delight.

From hiding secrets out of fear;

To revealing & admitting things with cheer.

From being emotionally stressed;

To being happily blessed.

We all secretly grown up from being a seed;

Transformed into a grown unique breed,

as humans performing good deeds.

_AditiAgarwal

Aditi Agarwal

10. <u>Mom</u>

The one that has been through so much of pain;
All through her veins.

When i was residing in her womb;
Considering it as my room.

When everthing turns up to a mess;
the sacrifice made by her becomes
Priceless.

Even the world is aware,
that a mom is known for the best care.

She's the one who works hard;
  As a family guard.

I love her shout;
When i pout.

Sometimes our opinions strife;
But she remains the mentor of my life.

My dad's wife;

Being the queen of his life.

Spending half of her day in cuisine;
Is her daily routine.

She is the one that plays multiple roles;
Being a single sole.

Sacrifice is another word for her life.

Out of all the rest,
Moms are the best.

_AditiAgarwal

30

11. *Dad*

He is the one who gave me birth;
He is the first man i knew on earth.

 I am glad;
 that i call him my dad.

He is the one who kept me
 away from all the dirt;
And gave me worth.

He is the one who get the smile on my face, whenever
i look sad;
I call him my beloved DAD.

_AditiAgarwal

32

12. *True Friend* 👫

Friendship is all about

companionship 👭

It has nothing to do with championship 🏆

A true friend will never pretend; to be a friend,

& will never let you descend.

Friendship is all about understanding 💯

that makes the bond even more outstanding.

A true friend will always defend your name,

& will never play double game.

A true friend never back-bitches;.

instead he/she takes all the wounds & heartbreaks

and stiches. 💔 💔 💔

A true friend remains the Same;

even after earning Fame. 💟

A true friend concerns everyday;

& leads you on to the right way. ⚲

A true friend will always stand by your side, 👭

Irrespective of it's Day or Night. 🌞 🌚

A true friend will always find one reason to stay, 👭

even if you give thousand of reasons to get away. 🙂

_AditiAgarwal

Aditi Agarwal

Nostalgia

Aditi Agarwal

13. <u>Childhood Days</u>

(THOSE WERE THE DAYS)

Those were the days,
when we were being loved in so many ways.

when our tears full of apprehension,
gained so much of attention.

Those were the days,
when we had a special craze,
to play with the molded clays.

All the pampering we used to acquire,
coz we were all so admired.

Deep inside in our minds, our memory conveys,
That those were the days,
when we were tensed free,.
& had no decisions on to agree.

All our memories that's perished,
could always be cherished.

Those were the days; when we had fun on,
also we had no worries to think upon.

At last; we could appraise,
All those childhood days.

Anyways:
We could not be sent back in those days,
but we can always feel & get lost in those precious
memorable moments & get back in   those times;
While expressing & getting through such Rhymes.

_AditiAgarwal

14. <u>A Child</u>

"A child is a gift of god,

a youth from a lord.

A little one from the maker

who's the creater of all.

A "human being",

from a " divine being".

_AditiAgarwal

Aditi Agarwal

15. The Delhi Trip

Planning for a trip,
appears to be so LIT.

All set with my kit,
along with my tucks & crisps.

When i get excite;
The more reasons i get to write & recite.

Suddenly, plan appears to slip,
but still, i tried my best to hold the grip.

WHAT NEXT?
Then i started getting more reasons to not Go,
but the little heart, still whispered: "To go with the flow."

what a situation to fuddle;
when everything appeared so puzzled.

NOW WHAT!?

I finally made a decision to not go & stay back.
& gave a confused look to my crisps bag.

wondering that all of those tucks and crisps

are now have become my evening snacks.

Apparantly; A thought tickled my mind;
that, all of my friends are having fun.

I firmly gave an excuse; they are under the sun,
might be feeling hot & getting burnt.

unlike me who can roam & run, grab a bun.
& that i too can have FUN.

Above all! There fun will always be lesser than my
mental satisfaction and the respect that i had for my
decision.

_AditiAgarwal

43

16. I Am Proud Of My School

Friendly, learning and cozy; the kind of
environment one would dream, where?
I studied there!

it's a place, where mentors work so hard,
that it is in itself a boon card.

we were bound to follow rules;
but i am proud of my school.

people do target the shortcomes;
and overlook the outcomes.

others might not be in the same pool,
but, I am proud of my school.

_AditiAgarwal

Current Scenario

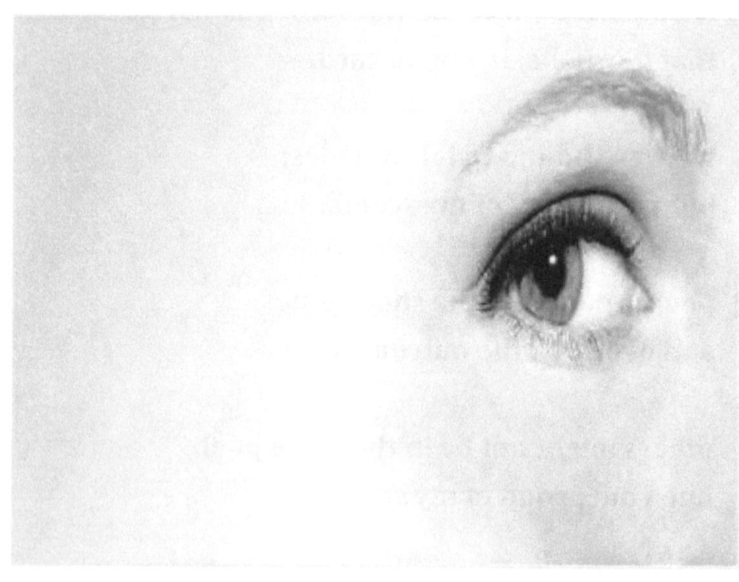

17. *Corona (2020)*

what a nature's woe!
when everything was apt, going with the flow.

A gust of catastrophe appeared,
and things got weird.

From all the accountants,
To all of the migrants.

Everybody encountered rage.
irrespective of their age.

wherein executives looked forward to provide the basic Assuages;
when all were kept imprisoned, with in their own respective homes, being cages.

what an international situation,
that stopped over all acceleration.

when people dealt with mental confusions,
apparantly, it lead to all of the family fusions.

Aditi Agarwal

what a misery, curse of nature,

that it couldn't be handled by any legislature.

Amazingly, it turns out to be a blessing in disguise,

that made our closed one's stay infront of our eyes. 👀

It brought our loved one's, so close to our heart,

that it will now become difficult to get apart.

The word "pandemic" what a nomenclature!

that it lead to the execution of everyone's amateur.

what a nature's fury!

that it decided to revisit it's lost glory.

while we live & try to see far;

there's horizon yet covered with covid scar.

wherein everything's been shut,

i wonder how did it happen so abrupt.

people wandering for shelter; all the migrants,

they are the ones who keep moving with aspirants.

An appeal to people within earth crust, 🌍

Do not let your determination, spirit & valour rust.

Because after every Dark night; ● ◎

there comes a morning with a sun bright. ☀ ⛰

let's all UNITE,
and wait for something to happen delight.

All we need is to keep ourselves SAFE.
& be a little brave.

QUIT ROAM! 🚐
STAY HOME.

_AditiAgarwal

Aditi Agarwal

18. Patriotism

(A Tribute To Our Dear Soldiers)

If soldiers would not have fought,
we would not have managed to sought.

Their courage to fight;
made our future bright.

Their devotion;
made our india on the heights of promotion.

We get tears,
when they leave the world without fears.

To all our dear soldiers, i contribute,
these words on behalf of my nation to give a tribute
with a salute.

Out of all the arts and stars,
our soldiers are the super stars.

AditiAgarwal

STOP
STOP
STOP
STOP
STOP
STOP
STOP
STOP
STOP
STOP
STOP
STOP
STOP

19. Quit Unnecessary Violence

Violence is something that is natural and it is the strongest form of an anger; it is said that it comes from within and could not be controlled or in other words the anger is not in our hands.

So, if your actions and emotions are not within your own control; how can you expect the situation or the person to be under your control.

It has been frequently noticed and could easily be seen in traffic prone areas, that if by mistake the auto, rikshaw puller or the person riding a bycycle hits up to your vehicle then people looses up the patience & control over their minds and they rush out of their cars to catch hold off that person.

The fight proceeds upto such an extent that it ends upto physical violence along with abusing; people feel privileged doing that because that person was the only one that could easily be dominated by them.

Violating him and abusing him might give you the mental satisfaction but just to let you aware that unnecessary violence takes you to the first step towards mental illness.

At the end of the situation your mental satisfaction will always be lesser than the criticism and bad deeds that will be released for you by his inner soul; at last at some point of time or the other, you (they) will be facing the same situation with reversed role personalities; cause at last nobody could ever escape from the lightning blaze of karma.

54

_AditiAgarwal

Basic Understanding

Aditi Agarwal

20. <u>*Being Yourself Vs Selfishness*</u>

Being yourself is cool, but turning selfish & stating that you are being yourself is fishy.

Uptill now we discussed about Being yourself but many or few would relate "Being yourself" with "selfishness". Though we need to understand both are two different things.

when it comes to being yourself, you think about yourself, you figure out how things could favour you as a whole, you think of creating your own happiness.

 But, when it comes to being selfish, there in that case you tend to only think about yourself, there, you try to figure out, how things could favour you in each specific situations, there you try to fulfill your greed for specific thing, irrespective of how others would feel.

now let's get into this and try to understand the basic difference through an example.

let's say, during class lectures, the teacher made an announcement which say's that the class representative has to be chosen, & it has to be between me and my friend.

now we are suppose to undergo a voting process in which, i voted for my friend and she voted for her ownself. now, everybody else jumped onto the conclusion that she's selfish & tried their best to convince me step against her, but i firmly explained, it's okay that she chose herself, everyone has different prospectives, different preferences, different opinions & different priorities, she wanted to be the class representative, so she chose herself, maybe that was her first preference & mine was to be happy in making her the class representative & bringing happiness to her way, what she did was absolutely right from her prospective, that's where we need to understand that she was being "herself" & not selfish.

Now what is selfishness?

let's understand this through a situation:

say, i and my friend went for our dance class, on that day, right after the dance class, my friend has to attend a birthday party, while dancing, i underwent leg injury, to which my friend reacted awkwardly and said that she will catch me later as she has to attend the birthday party.

now, here we need to understand the selfishness behind this, she left, irrespective of knowing the fact that her friend has unknowingly injured herself, still; she went to attend the birthday party. That's where we recognise selfishness.

_AditiAgarwal

My Place

21. Ego Vs Self-Respect

Self respect is to know your self worth & understand as to what behaviour you deserve along with self-esteem.

whereas, Ego refers to overlook things, that you think you deserve, wherein you exaggerate self-conceit.

And therefore, having self-respect is honourable however, becoming egoistic with the name sake of self-respect is peculiar.

Both are two different aspects which are usually mistinterpretated with the agnomen of having self-respect.

Hence, it's very important to learn and understand the exact difference between ego & self-respect.

Let's understand this with an example:

let's say It's my friend's birthday:

but, "my friend didn't wished me, so am also not going to wish her."

(This kind of mind-set reflects: that the person is being egoistic & has taken revenge.)

example for self-respect:

let's say It's my birthday, i wished her on her birthday but seems like, she forgot my birthday; However, am not going to remind her of my birthday, otherwise it would question my self-respect.

let's get more clear with this through another example:

let's say

The teacher asked myra and kyra to collaborate together and work for a project.

Mind-set of Myra : Am not going to approach her first, i am going to wait for her to come and approach me first.

(This kind of mindset clearly reflects Ego, this is being egoistic)

Mind set of Kyra: Every time it's me to approach her first but for this time, am not going to go & approach her first.

(This kind of mindset reflects self-respect)

I hope now the difference is quite clear between both the two aspects of Ego and self-respect, if you still are stuck on to what is going to happen in that collaboration, one needs to let go off their ego in order to achieve something in life. so with this let's quit all our ego here itself and look forward to nurture our thoughts and brains with postivity.

_AditiAgarwal

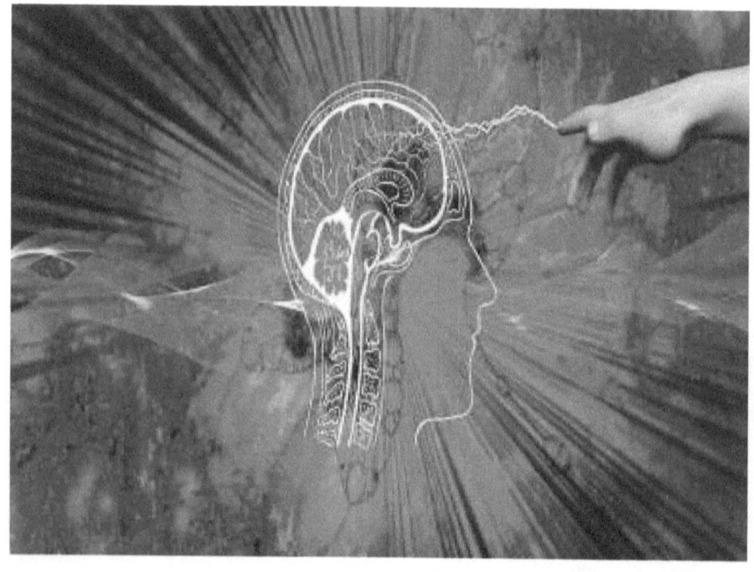

22. Misinterpretation Of Self Importance

There is a misconception about self importance as its generally overlooked & misinterpretated with seeking attention.

let's say,

your friends have made a plan for a club party tonight and when they asked you to join in the party.

now for this a very genuine reply could be:

1. (inner voice says): It will be fun, will have great time.

reply with this mind-set: yes, why not, it will be fun, we will have great time.

(This kind of mindset reflects respectful nature, as the person is respecting the decision made by his/her friends.)

Now several other replies with different mind-sets are:

2. (inner voice says): They should have included me while making the plan itself, it's like they have made

the plans and now after making it they are asking me afterwards to join as if i have got no importance.

reply with this mind-set: No, you should have discussed the plan with me while making itself, i have got my self importance, & I don't stay in the absence of my selfimportance.

(This kind of mindset reflects egoistic nature)

3. (inner voice says): Now that they have already made the plans and knowing that anyhow, they will be going let me see if i have got any self importance, let me see if they urge & force me to join in.

reply with this mind-set: No, i am not willing   to join in. (or some other excuse to see if they urge me to join in)

(This kind of mind-set reflects attention seeking nature, the person thought that by rejecting the plan it will create my self importance & it would make my friends urge me to join in at the party.)

Now, this is not what is known to be as self importance; This is seeking importance which makes no good to a person.

your self importance is for your ownself, which you need to create within your inner-self and you need not ask for it from others as it's not something that you should seek for it.

when you genuinely have some other reason to be not able to join in , say you already have some other plans with your family for tonight.

4. (inner voice says): ohno! have to go for dinner tonight with my family.

 reply with this mind-set: sorry, i already had my plans for tonight with my family, but no worries, will join in next time for sure.

(This mind-set reflects out to be natural and genuine personality. shows kind and apologistic nature, polite way of speaking. utilised self imprtortance correctly.)

The first and foremost thing is to have a clear mind-set, here: in this case the person had to make a decision and understand the priorities and choose one between family and friends, the ultimate decision that came out to be family and was fair enough as it had been pre-planned. now here the way you speak or reply reflects your nature, your personality and your prioritisation reflects your self importance.

The other way out of giving a reply for the same situation could be somewhat like:

"No, i have my family dinner tonight and that's more important to me than this party."

now the clear difference is just of the way you speak, & that is all what exactly matters.
self importance is for your own inner-self that need not to be extracted & outrated.

_AditiAgarwal

Aditi Agarwal

23. Realise Before It's Too Late

Okay, so let's understand one thing, we all have that one person in our life, whom we dislike, or we say, that "i hate him/her" okay, am not using this strong word hate, let's just say we dislike someone, and am sure we all have that specific person in our life, whom we do not like. Now, my point is, let's just say, like god forbid, nobody wants that to happen, but just thinking of the worst, just imagine that person is no more.

Take a pause & think, how are you going to react to it, what are you going to feel at that time, you know, you won't even have a mixed feeling, but you will just feel sad, you will be in greif.

Am sure none of you are going to react favouring the situation, saying that person deserved not to be alive & feel good.

Now, we need to understand what left us in grief, you know what, no matter what kind of relation you shared with that person, but you will feel apologistic, & you will see yourself being in deep guilt, inspite of you hated or disliked that person, still you won't feel good. now ask yourself WHY? is it because you need someone to dislike. No, it's just you will land up recalling all the positivity within that person, you will recall all the good deeds made by the person, the conclusion is you will just only see the positive side of that person, & you will come across having this realisation only after that person has left you, when you will understand the fact that you won't ever meet that person again, & that person is gone. now my point is why do we need to wait for this realisation to hit us & leave in deep greif. when we have good amount of time in our life to like & appreciate each one we meet. Nobody is perfect, we all are imperfectly flawed, & that is all we need to cherish.

REALISE BEFORE IT'S TOO LATE.
APOLOGISE BEFORE IT'S TOO LATE.
LOVE BEFORE IT'S TOO LATE.

AditiAgarwal

24. *Spread Love And Positivity All Around* ♡ ♥ ♥ ♡

People who treats you good, treat them good.

people who love you, love them back.

people who dislikes you, give them reasons to like you.

people who hate you, never hate them back, just pray for them to get healed.

let's have a look at a situation below:

let's say, kyra & myra are two friends.

one day, Kyra betrayed Myra, which broke Myra from inside, badly & she started hating kyra for what she did.

Now, kyra is left with two options:

1. first option was to stuck on to what she did & favour herself, by stating what she did was justified.

2. second option, was to realise her own mistake, & apologize to Myra.

now, what option would you go with? in this situation, many of you would say that, it depends on to the exact situation as to what kyra did to Myra, i say let it be anything, or assume the worst you could think of, she could have done.

My point is, she was hurt, and that's enough to convince me, onto go with the second option.

because we need to understand that hurting & hating are directly proportional to each other, when you get hurt, you start hating.

when hurting increases, hating also tends to rise.

The only way you could prevent yourself from being hated, is to always heal up the hurted soul and never hate or hurt them back.

Life goes on one rule of KARMA.

once, you give something, you get in return.

whatsoever & anything you give, you get it reverted.

when we talk about appreciation. we want appreciation endlessly, but let's ask a question to ourselves, that are we also pro at giving appreciation & complements endlessly? The answer would come: No, in majority.

Then why do we expect those things from others in which we ourselves lack in giving.

Start pulling people upwards, instead of pushing them & digging pits for others to fall, because at the end you will find your ownself in it. For living a peaceful life, We need to Learn to give respect, love, care & help others.

This will spread love & positivity all around.

LIFE IS, A CYCLE OF WHAT YOU GIVE OTHERS, YOU RECEIVE IT.

74

_AditiAgarwal

25. Do You Hate Anyone?

If yes, Then why do all fall in love with that same person, who when receives a call from heaven, i don't understand one thing we all have one life, let's cherish all what we have, all the beautiful souls that we have in the form of our friends & family coz our life is really short but it's we who need to make it live long, live & enjoy the every bit of your moment, why do we need to hate someone when we have enough of love to give away, Also, we never know, when & where we could end up meeting a person for the very last time, All the one's that you have interacted with, do make sure, you leave a good remark in their books of good deeds, because one or the other day, karma settles well, everyone's account of good and bad deeds.

AditiAgarwal

26. *Knowledge*

The value of knowledge
cannot be measured;

but it could only be treasured!

The value of knowledge can not be sold;
but it's a wealth that one can hold.

Knowledge cannot be bought;

But it could only be, learned and taught.
Gaining extra knowledge never harms;

But it's just a way to keep one's mind calm.

Knowledge is like a boon flower which is always
cherished,
& Could never get perish.

From The Basket Of Love

"Dear girls"
"if you have to sacrifice your self-respect,
for becoming a miss Perfect,
then understand, your Mr. is not perfect!"

_AditiAgarwal

RESPECT
RESPECT
RESPECT
RESPECT
RESPECT
RESPECT
RESPECT
RESPECT
RESPECT
RESPECT
RESPECT
RESPECT
RESPECT
RESPECT
RESPECT
RESPECT
RESPECT

27. *Respect Her Beyond Loving Her*

start appreciating, what you have,

instead of appreciating other's ex.

coz when you don't appreciate her today,

she, maynot even grass you, the other day.

learn to Admire & Appreciate your own girl,

untill she changes her way to people who, admire her,
value her presence & dream to have her.

There are many other guys, she can easily turn her
way to; who wipes her tear off, when she get those
teary eyes, from you.

 But that's not her way to sly on, because however, she
remains a loyal bitch, until

 You admire someother girl more.

She then tends to admire you, a little lesser,

by admiring her ownself, even a little more.

when you can't treat her like your queen,

never expect her to treat you, like a king.

learn to respect her feelings, stop outrating other's ex.

that won't ever make her feel complex.

because she values & admires herself more than
anything in this world,

that's how, a psycho lover she's when it comes to
herself.

understand, when she can be psycho, & get madly inlove with herself, how true her love would be, when it comes, for the only men of her life.

The day, you will start admiring girls, other than her.

 Each day, you will loose her, a little more.

when time passes by, you would be shaken to know & realise the fact of loosing a precious gem, that you once ever had.

_Aditi Agarwal

"Dear girls"

Fall for a guy, who is in love with your beautiful heart & respects your opinions and not the one who is a well "sugar quotted" speaker, who loves your outer looks & outer beauty.

AditiAgarwal

28. *Short Love Story*♡♡
(*True Love Never Dies*)

They fell in love with each other at the age of fifteen;
There love for each other made them self esteem.

They left no chance to have a fight;
But the knowt of true love was tied very tight.♡

Since they fell in love at an early age;
The parents & society didn't approved their love.

So, They were made apart from
eachother;
But only the two hearts knew that they were a part of
eachother.♡

They always stood at each other's side;
With a pride.♡

According to their parents and society,
the only fault they made was to love eachother at an
early age;
But, their love for each other was a rage.(craze)

Under parents pressure;

All they could do was to hide their love for each other like a treasure.

Years passed; nothing got changed,

Except the decision of disapproval;

later, they got married,

& their love for each other was now cherished.

_AditiAgarwal

love has got no space for competition, if the person you love talks about being in competition, or wants to be your competitor, then understand, that the person never loved you because competition is held between two lives. but, love is all about "one life - two soul".

AditiAgarwal

29. A Letter To God

God give me mercy
to be with me.
God give me talent,
to build a Graceland.
God give me treasure,
full of manners.
God give me courage,
to accept my mistake.
God help me to speak the truth,
to be good with my youth.
God help me to rule the world,
with truth, care, justice, kindness and happiness.

_AditiAgarwal

"Be a person whom, others give attention, & that you never have to seek for someone's attention, if you are an attention seeker, understand your presence makes no difference, but if you get attention without seeking it, know that you are precious."

_AditiAgarwal